Santa Visits

NOT WHAT YOU EXPECT

T0025398

Santa Visits

NOT WHAT YOU EXPECT

DAVID CHILD

TATE PUBLISHING
AND **ENTERPRISES**, LLC

Published by Tate Publishing & Enterprises, LLC
127 E. Trade Center Terrace | Mustang, Oklahoma 73064 USA
1.888.361.9473 | www.tatepublishing.com

Tate Publishing is committed to excellence in the publishing industry. The company reflects the philosophy established by the founders, based on Psalm 68:11,
"The Lord gave the word and great was the company of those who published it."

Book design copyright © 2014 by Tate Publishing, LLC. All rights reserved.
Cover design by Jim Villaflores
Interior design by Gram Telen
Illustrations by Charlo Nocete

Published in the United States of America

ISBN: 978-1-62854-117-5
1. Fiction / Holidays
2. Fiction / General
14.02.12

Acknowledgment

Serious thanks to my wife, Vicky. Her patience and incredible writing skills added so much quality to this work.

Jim McGinniss, author of *Jimmy's OTHER Glove* (Tate), volunteered much appreciated encouragement and momentum.

Lilian Edwards, Katia Alves-Edgar, and Dale Mayes were used as unsuspecting test-subjects as the drafts were being developed. Their responses and comments were invaluable.

Superb web management by BADCAT DESIGN, New Hope, Pennsylvania—thank you, Kel!

The unbelievably professional staff at Tate Publishing…wow! I can't start to express my thankfulness for the pure joy of this experience. But I'll try!

Dear Katie and Edward,

I'm writing to you both as my dear cousins. Unusual things have been happening in my life recently.

If you will, read on. Perhaps then you might tell me what you think.

Some Unusual Things

*E*very year as time gets close to Christmas, here in the Village of New Hope, at the end of our working days, nighttime becomes very cold and very dark—actually, very, very dark and bitter, bitter cold. That's our midwinter nights. We like to stay inside.

On this particular cold, winter night I was the only person left behind working at the printing shop. I was there because of a problem with a big, honking, clunking printing machine that would not honk, clunk, or even print. Although the machine needed to be fixed quickly, I couldn't seem to find the problem. Instead, I planned that I would head home to our warm fireplace and a hot supper and, then, tomorrow see what I could do.

But this was one Christmas Eve when the unexpected was to be my future. Late into the evening, as I was turning off all the lights and as I was just about to lock the back door, I heard a huge amount of noise outside: clattering, banging, crashing, and, then, coughing, wheezing, and sneezing. It was all a little bit odd, but I knew I had to take a look. I pushed the back door open just a little and peered out into the night.

It was there*! It was there!* I couldn't believe my eyes! I had heard all about it but never, ever, thought I would see it.

The Santa Claus sleigh, brilliantly bright, beautiful and colorfully sleek in the dark, dark night. A fast flying machine.

What I was seeing was like a fairy tale. *There it was…*standing next to my back door shimmering and colorful as could be. Dazzling! Eight reindeers were all shaking their heads and scratching their hooves on the ground, snorting and snuffing the way, I think, reindeers might normally do, twitching their tails and looking like they couldn't wait to be back flying through the sky. In the dark night, the deer and the sleigh gleamed brightly. The deer were sleek, golden brown, with their fur glistening in the moonlight. As I stepped through the door, they all looked at me with big brown eyes. They stopped scratching the hard ground. Silently and with perfect stillness, they stood and looked—no sound, no fear, just curiosity.

Although the reindeer and the sleigh were there, I was surprised that Santa Claus was nowhere to be seen. Getting over my nervousness a little more, I ventured further outside. It was bitterly cold and dark. The chill went through my clothes in a second, and I couldn't help but start to shiver immediately. Again, the reindeer began to paw the ground, shook themselves to throw off the cold, and made the shiny sleigh shake back and forth slightly, just enough to jingle the silver bells.

I heard a cough, then two, then three, and then a sneeze. Around the back of the sleigh I found…Santa Claus!

He was hunched over the edge of the sleigh and holding a huge paper towel to his nose.

"Sir," I said, "can I help you?"

Santa seemed a little grumpy. He complained that he had a cold and that a cold on this Christmas Eve night definitely wasn't acceptable.

"Can't have a cold when you have to fly all around the world. Makes your ears pop when we start flying, and then after that, your nose sneezes!" he grumbled.

It was confusing to me, but I said, "I thought that every sentence Santa Claus spoke started with "Ho, ho, ho!"

"Tonight," he said, "it's more like no, no, no!"

"Would it help," I asked, "if you came inside for a few minutes and had a cup of tea?"

Santa Claus turned slowly and looked directly at me. "I'll try it out, my friend, if you don't mind."

I walked to the door. It's big, steel, and *very* heavy. We pushed the door open, and Santa Claus stepped inside.

I made him hot tea with sugar and milk in a big, green mug. Santa sat in a large chair and put his feet up on the table. He sighed a huge, big sigh and sipped his tea. He seemed happier.

Santa spoke, "I hate catching a cold in winter. Most inconvenient! Much better if it's in the summer. I just fly the sleigh south to a warm

place and sit in the sun on a beach. Kills off the cold in two days."

I strained trying not to chuckle!

He paused and looked around. "The tea is good. I'm feeling much better." He added, "But what are you doing here so late on Christmas Eve?"

"One of our printing machines is not working," I answered, pointing to my problem.

Santa looked at the cantankerous machine and frowned.

"That machine should be honking and clunking," he observed.

"Yes, sir," I said. "I'll try to fix it tomorrow because I have to deliver some print work next day."

"Fix it? On Christmas day?" he bellowed and waved his arms quite energetically. "That's not good enough, and it doesn't seem right!"

Then, more quietly, he said, "You could do with a little favor."

"Anything would help. This is very important. I hope I can figure the problem out."

Santa Claus was looking more relaxed. I suddenly thought of the reindeer outside and offered to take some water.

I stepped back into the cold night with a bucket of clear fresh water. The deer, waiting there, were even more restless, still eager to fly. The first deer, Lead'Deer, gratefully took a long drink of water and then passed the bucket to the next reindeer. *Passed the bucket! How do reindeer pass a bucket? I watched it! I saw it! I could not believe my eyes.*

Shaking my head at this magical sight, I walked back inside.

Santa Claus was almost napping, but he woke as soon as I stepped through the door.

"I wish," he said quietly, "that everyone could celebrate Christmas at Christmas but, even more, would continue to spread the goodness and giving throughout the year. I think everyone would be happier, and it would be a small gift to me."

He laughed softly. "Especially when I have a cold."

"You deserve a gift, Santa."

"It could be that I just received one," he said. "Nice cup of tea...clean drinking water... friendship."

He stood, stretched his arms and legs, and said, "Must get flying. Don't forget to give small gifts when they are least expected and attach love always."

"Thanks for the hot tea and the water for my reindeer. Your kindness will be remembered."

In an instant, Santa Claus disappeared. Immediately, I heard the impatient reindeer and jingling sleigh swoop upward into the winter sky. The sound of them taking off was musical, almost like a harp and a small trumpet playing together with the tiny shining bells.

I stood in silence.

The lights I had turned off earlier had not been turned back on during this whole visit, so I was now in complete darkness. It was unbelievably hard to understand what I had just experienced. Children are told about Santa Claus and reindeer that can fly and gifts to all good children, all good people. I had just seen it all, the whole wondrous tale.

Suddenly, in the dark silence, there was a surprising and welcome noise!

Large motors started humming and electronic lights started flashing rapidly—red, yellow, green! A cacophony of machine sounds: honking and clunking, the broken printing

machine was back in operation and running…
all on its own!

Even more amazing: The first piece of paper that came out was a beautiful color picture…of Santa Claus!

The machine was operating at full speed, powered by some invisible force, and I could see that my big printing job would be finished very quickly this night. I looked again at the picture of Santa Claus, *and it spoke to me with a smile:* "Thank you, my friend. Small favor returned. Ho, ho, ho!"

The picture slowly changed to snowflakes that drifted to the floor.

As they were falling, Santa's last word reached me: "Believe."

Easily Surprising

The second time I met Santa Claus was easily as surprising as the first.

The evening was a perfectly beautiful end to a perfectly beautiful summer day. I walked outside and gazed up at the sky. *Delightful.* Long strings of white fluffy clouds below a light blue sky. *Very pleasant.*

To my left, I noticed some dark and heavy thunder clouds were moving quickly toward our village. It was one of those summer storms that would be with us soon. Stone, gray clouds rolled and churned. Lightning flashed brightly from cloud to cloud, crackling down to the ground. Deep, loud thunder followed.

I looked at the blue and white sky to my right and the contrast of the incoming storm to my left.

Then…something *else* caught my eye.

In the front of the dark, churning storm clouds was a fast moving brilliance, like a large, silver comet. The glowing object weaved from left to right and back to left. It swooped up and dove down. Suddenly, it curved away from the front of the storm and raced in my direction. It became larger and larger as it aimed directly at me like a speeding bullet!

As the mysterious radiance drew closer, its silver color started to change. Like the distant autumn, it became red, green, and golden brown. A faint musical sound reached my ears. It was… like a harp, tiny bells, and a small trumpet!

The sleigh! Santa Claus and eight golden reindeer were rushing toward me at impossible speed. They flew down to within feet of my head and then curved up high into the sky. The deer and sleigh disappeared behind my building, but I could still hear the music of their flight—fainter and fainter, almost to silence, and then louder again until, as I looked up, the deer and sleigh swooped inches over the top of the building, a huge, racing, flying machine. Santa Claus steered around, upside down, and then flew in sideways toward the ground. The deer and sleigh skidded broadside onto the ground with lots of noise and sparks and scraping. The sleigh jumped and bumped and almost toppled over before it came to an abrupt stop.

Santa Claus was delighted! He was laughing uncontrollably: "Ho, ho, and *ho!*" He was obviously in a playful mood.

"What terrific fun!" he shouted. "Almost as good as doughnuts in the snow! Ho, ho, ho!"

The reindeer were not quite so amused. Their hooves hurt from the rough landing, and they all stared at Santa Claus with displeasure.

Santa jumped lightly off his sleigh and hugged the reindeer—all of them—one at a time. They spoke, quietly, for a few moments. The reindeer relaxed and even smiled a little.

I felt at a loss for what I might do. Remembering Santa's first visit, I offered water.

"Good idea," said Santa. "I'll relax and enjoy the sunshine."

He took his red jacket off and sat on the grass, crossed his legs, smiled, and faced the setting sun.

I brought water to the deer, and they took care of themselves, as before.

I was strolling toward Santa, and he spoke to me, "Beautiful evening."

"Look at that gorgeous storm moving to the east. Perfect ride!"

"I like thunderstorms too," I told Santa. "But what do you mean about *riding*?"

"Like a wave. You see the front clouds of that storm? High, rolling, and moving forward fast. Pick your spot high, and ride it like a surfboard on the ocean. Great fun! You would love it!"

"Santa, sir, I could not sit in an open sleigh swooping around the sky. I would simply fall out and crash, down onto the ground, who knows where!"

"You might enjoy being introduced to my sleigh," Santa said with a wink and a smile. "Jump in, and make yourself comfortable. I will have a short conversation with the deer."

He sprang up from the grass like an athlete and walked over to wrap his arms around the neck of the Lead'Deer. They spoke for a short time as I walked slowly and a little nervously to the sleigh. I climbed on board and sat on Santa's seat. It was very large and comfortable. I stared at the reins hanging in front of me and sensed that I should not touch them.

"Forget the reins!" Santa shouted as though he could read my mind. "The deer will steer. You can relax and do nothing or, if you want to, just call up, down, left, or right or anything else that you want. You'll be fine. Ready to go?"

"Sir, I might fall out!"

The deer rose a foot off the ground and so did the sleigh. We were floating with nothing below us, nothing at all!

Santa stood alongside.

"So you are airborne," he said. "Not moving, but above the ground! *Airborne!*"

I looked over the side of the sleigh at the ground just below.

"Yes, sir, just a little."

"Very good," Santa said. "Try to stand up."

I tried, but nothing happened. It was as though I was strapped into the sleigh. I sat looking at Santa as he looked back at me.

"This will happen when you get up there. Maybe even more so." He chuckled.

I was trying to find the courage to say that maybe it would be all right to fly when Santa suddenly shouted, "Go!"

The reindeer's hooves churned up gravel and crackling sparks. The sleigh shot forward at breathtaking speed. I fell backward into Santa's seat.

"You'll be okay!" I heard as we took off. "You will be surprised at what you will find."

Within a minute, the sleigh and I were thousands of feet in the air. We raced to the east. Just before the New York City skyline, we spun completely around and rushed toward the approaching storm. It was incredibly beautiful but fearsome as well. Clouds with the color of charcoal were rolling as high as I could see. Across the top was a narrow strip of gold as the sun tried to peer over the challenging storm.

We flew to within just an arm's reach of the storm. I could lean sideways and touch it. It was a breathtaking sight to behold from so close— the thickness, the churning, and the clashing of thunder and lightning.

In front of the clouds was a most peculiar tangle of light, golden-brown strings, intertwined and interwoven like a loose flowing fabric net, trying to capture the storm and all its power. The reindeer steered directly into the magical net until I could feel the strings brush across my face. They were soft, gentle, and pleasant as they wrapped around me. It was a comfortable and safe feeling. I could hear the strings humming softly. As I was enjoying the experience, the sleigh rose high above the storm leaving my cocoon behind.

The Lead'Deer turned to me.

"Are you safe?" she asked. "Raise your hand if you are."

I couldn't. The seat held me securely in place, so she knew I was safe.

She nodded her approval. "Let's ride."

"Ride!" I exclaimed. But it was too late.

The reindeer team spun around in the sky, and I saw the world slipping by until I was looking straight down at the ground below. As we turned upright again, I knew the real surfing was about to begin.

Our dive started gradually but gained speed quickly. We rode at an angle through the strings, with the storm clouds rushing and pushing us forward. We bumped and bounced and raced like I could never have imagined at ten thousand feet above the ground!

My heart raced, my head spun, and I was soaked in sweat! It was exhilarating! It was the most thrilling experience ever.

We reached the bottom of the clouds and flew beneath the churning storm power with lightning and thunder crashing and booming just feet above. A wave of heavy rain suddenly soaked us. I was drenched and starting to feel cold.

The Lead'Deer turned her head to me. "Are you cold?" she asked kindly.

I shivered a little and nodded my head.

"Time to warm up."

She guided us back above the storm into the warm sunshine. We hovered a few feet above the raging storm clouds. I looked down at the powder white, fluffy clouds and thought how strange it was that just below those clouds was so much darkness, rain, and crashing and flashing lightning. How odd it had felt to be able to surf the front of a storm. I thought of the exciting ride and called out to the deer, "Let's do it again!"

And so we did.

Afterward we decided to land.

Santa Claus had not moved one inch. He remained seated, cross-legged, on the grass smiling at the sun.

We glided in on our approach, and he opened his eyes to watch. We touched down, smoothly and softly. The deer nodded their approval. *Much better landing this time!*

"Had fun, did you?" he asked.

I took a deep breath and then exhaled loudly. "Unbelievable!"

"Believe," he said quietly with a twinkle in his eyes.

Santa walked around the sleigh and hugged each of the deer again.

"When you are hugging, there is nothing between you, only love and honesty."

He reached the back of the sleigh.

"What a treat!" he said emphatically. "This almost never happens!"

I didn't understand but was curious.

Santa explained, "Golden-brown, flowing strands from the storm front caught in the sleigh's runner. They are still humming."

"Ho, ho! Watch this."

I looked. I watched. But I could not see. Santa's hands moved so quickly it was in a blur.

When he stopped, he said, "I'm done. It's yours."

Santa held up a perfect braid of storm strings. He started to hand it to me but suddenly changed his mind. He spread it wide around my head and placed it comfortably on my neck.

Very quietly I heard a gentle hum from the strings. The evening continued to be most pleasant.

How Lucky Could I Be?

*I*t was fall, later in the year. And it was a beautiful day. Trees were adorned with leaves of gold, scarlet, chocolate, and brilliant orange. I was walking through all this beauty. *How lucky could I be?*

I love to fish. I know a certain special place where fishing is, I think, unbelievably good. I had gathered my fishing pole and canvas bag filled with a sandwich, bottle of water, and fishing equipment. I hiked through nearly a half mile of thick, beautiful forest and prickly brush.

It is a small lake completely surrounded by hills, trees, and brush to the water's edge. There is just one small, stony beach. I find my way there tree by tree.

I have never seen anyone at the lake. There has never been anyone on the small, stony beach. On this day, I pushed my way through the brush to the stony beach and stepped out in front of the water to see a very large man in a checkered shirt and faded, old jeans.

I hesitated for a moment and stood still. The large man slowly turned around and looked directly at me. He smiled a big smile. I recognized him immediately.

"Santa Claus!" I was so excited to see him again.

"How are you my friend?" he asked loudly.

"I'm well, sir. How are you? What brings you to this place?"

"I looked at my list and had a good idea that you might be heading this way. So I thought I might come to meet you."

"A pleasure, Santa. Can I do anything for you?"

Santa Claus paused and looked over the water. He sighed at the beauty.

"This is so perfect. How did you find it?

"Accidentally. My friend owns an antique airplane. He takes me for rides occasionally. The plane flies low and slow. One day, we flew

over this pond, and I knew I had to find it from down on the ground. So I searched and searched, then after a while found myself right here where we stand."

"The fishing is good, I can tell," he said.

"As good as you might believe!"

"Ho, ho, ho! Believe," he repeated.

Santa coughed a quiet little cough. He raised his hand to his mouth, tapped his forehead, and then turned his head away from me.

"You asked if you could help, and you can, if you agree. It's up to you."

"Anything, Santa. Whatever I can do for you."

"Although they are all around us, you don't usually see fairies, do you?"

"I've never seen even one, sir."

"Happily, they are very secretive."

He paused.

"Fairies become adults in thirteen days after they are born."

He paused again.

"I have a friend with a damaged wing. If we don't fix her wing very quickly, she will not become an adult, and she will not be able to fly where she wants to fly or lift off her wings and walk where she pleases.

"She is twelve days and eleven hours old right now with a torn wing she caught on a thorn. I know how to repair her wing, but I need your help."

My help? I couldn't believe I could do anything. But I said to Santa, "Anything."

"Your braid of storm strings," Santa said.

"Your gift to me?"

"May I take back a few inches, please?"

Without hesitation, I lifted the treasured strand over my head and passed it to Santa Claus. He quickly loosened and snipped a short piece, then repaired the braiding. In a moment, it was placed back around my neck.

"I'm sorry, but thunderstorms are becoming out of season, and we didn't have a source of strings. That's why I came to you. Are your strings still vibrating?"

"Softly," I answered.

"Perfect," he replied. "I must get back to help the fairy, but first…" Santa clipped the last inch from the humming string.

Then he reached into one of his large jacket pockets and pulled and tugged until a complete fishing pole slowly emerged. At the end of the fishing line was a large hook.

"We shouldn't use storm strings too often like this; however, once in a while is okay."

Santa tied the last piece of the vibrating golden string to the hook and tossed it into the water. Fishes raced to it. Immediately, he had a large one on the line. He caught it and handed it to me.

"I must fix the fairy's wing. I'm sure she will come to thank you."

Santa walked into the woods and silently disappeared as he moved through the brush. I stayed on the stony beach and thought about fishing. *What else should I do?* I ate my sandwich. It was a beautiful fall day. Slowly, I fell asleep. The sun was warm and comfortable. It was very pleasant.

There was a fluttering, tickling feeling on my cheek. I awoke with a start.

"Oh!" I heard, and the fluttering moved away.

I opened my eyes and saw a most beautiful sight.

She was no more than three inches tall, in a white gown decorated with delicate colorful flowers. Flowers were also in her hair and wrapped around her wrists and ankles. Her wings were white with colorful shades of pink,

green, and brown. One wing had a golden string stitched repair.

She hovered a foot in front of me.

"I came to thank you," she said. "I might not have made it to thirteen days."

"I did little. Just gave back some strings."

"It was everything to me. When I reach thirteen days old, I become a complete fairy!"

"That truly makes me happy," I answered.

She smiled.

"I slept too long here by the water. Now I think I need to head back home."

I stood and started walking back through the woods.

The fairy fluttered alongside me as I struggled through the thick undergrowth.

One of the reasons the fishing pond is so private is that there is a very steep hill that must be climbed to get there and climbed down again to leave. I reached the hill and started my descent.

Suddenly, the ground below crumbled. I started to fall! I grabbed at a tree branch. The branch and the tree fell with me and tumbled to the bottom of the hill.

There at the bottom I lay on the ground looking at the sky. The tree lay on top of me; it was heavy and painful. I couldn't move.

She flew there right next to me.

"What can I do?" she asked.

I was bruised and hurt.

"My canvas bag…over there. Can you pull my cell phone out?"

She flew to the bag and struggled to pull the phone out. A cell phone is big and heavy for a fairy, but she pulled it out into the open.

"Please dial 911," I said. "Please."

"I will have to jump on the phone keys to make them work."

She walked away from the phone, turned around, and sprinted back. She leaped into the air so that she could land on the first key. The breeze caught her wings, and she drifted away to the side. She tried again but with the same result. The third try also failed.

"I wish I was thirteen. I could take my wings off," she said.

"Santa Claus said you were close to thirteen. Would you try?"

She tugged and pulled. She squirmed and wriggled and gasped. A wing came loose and then the second. She became thirteen days old! She became an adult fairy! The new fairy placed her wings carefully beneath a small stone.

Aiming at the cell phone, she leaped on the nine key and then the other twice.

A voice answered, "Do you need help? Keep your phone on, and we will find you."

They found me, and in less than an hour, I was in a hospital bed completely comfortable.

I lay peacefully when I felt a fluttering close by. *The fairy's wings.*

"How are you?" she asked.

"I'm well. I'll be home tomorrow."

"I owe you everything. You helped me become a fairy. I will always be your friend."

"I did little, but I also owe you much," I replied.

She came close to me and kissed my cheek. She blew softly on my forehead.

"Fairy dust," she said. "You can't ever see it, but any time you need me say my name three times. I'll be with you."

"But…I don't know your name." I was falling asleep.

"When you need my name, you will know it."

She flew away.

When I awoke, the rescue chief was standing by my bed, uniformed, smart, upright, and professional.

"Just checking on how you are doing, sir," he said. "You are looking fine."

I nodded and said, "Thank you."

The chief continued, "Just wondering, professionally, sir, and maybe personally. With a tree across your chest, how you did you dial and answer your cell phone so far out of your reach?"

"Chief, thank you so much for helping me. How was the phone dialed? Sir, please…*believe*."

Toes

The next time I met Santa Claus was another complete surprise. It was springtime, more than a year after I first met him.

I was sitting alone. The bank of the Delaware Canal is a wonderful place to admire daffodils in bloom, surrounded by trees and bushes all in flowering glory. It was a beautiful evening laced with the melodies of an orchestra of birds and crickets. A warm breeze gently swayed. The foliage seemed to dance. It was possibly one of my favorite places in the world—quiet, peaceful, and perfect. I was ready to take a comfortable nap when a huge voice bellowed from behind me, "What a great day!"

Startled, I almost jumped and spilled into the water. Grabbing the reed grass on the bank and a branch from a tree, I caught myself. I turned to see Santa Claus striding in my direction.

Santa Claus is a big person, as you might know—several feet tall and somewhat wide. But he strides in complete silence through dry leaves, wet grass, or fallen tree branches and twigs and even snow with big, long steps. Sometimes when walking in the woods, I've noticed, he simply disappears into thin air!

On this day, Santa was dressed in a gray sweat suit. He walked over to me.

"Nice day. Isn't it?" he said loudly.

I was still startled but remained quiet. I have learned to trust this spontaneous friend of mine, but I suspected that something just *might* be coming up.

Santa sat on the canal bank next to me. He pulled off his big boots and socks, then plunged his feet into the cool, dark water.

He wriggled his toes and swished his feet.

"How are things going?" he asked, kindly.

"Well, Santa, as you said, it's a great day."

"A great day," repeated Santa Claus.

He and I sat side by side in silence for a long time. We looked at the water, watching fish and turtles slowly swimming by. A stately heron waded nearby, cautiously peering and stalking, one step at a time, searching for a small feast.

"You must be off duty, sir. No red suit, no reindeer. Is it vacation for you?"

"I get the occasional day off," Santa replied. "Gaze at water, sometimes meet with a friend."

"A day off for me might sound nice," I answered. "Perhaps with a little adventure, but I don't seem to find the time to do it as often as I'd like."

We continued to sit quietly, Santa and me, and then, to my surprise (ever present in Santa's company), a fairy flew gently in front of us.

She fluttered and danced in the air and then landed on Santa's knee.

"Your feet are in the water," the fairy said to him.

"They are," Santa answered.

"You are wriggling your toes."

Santa chuckled. "I am."

"Exertoezes," the fairy said. "It will work. You will feel well."

She sat on his knee, looking over the canal.

The fairy sighed a small sigh. "Exertoezes."

Santa continued to wriggle his toes in the gently moving waters of the canal.

I looked at the fairy.

"I think I know you. Your wing has healed completely."

She smiled at me, then watched a daffodil flower admiring the sunshine.

"My wing is all better now. For me, this is a special place!" she confided.

"Special?" I asked.

"Special. Always," she answered. "My wing is well. You are here. So this is a special place."

Santa coughed. "Just an idea," he said. "On the subject of adventures, there may be possibilities available. Ho, ho?" He paused a moment. "You have surfed clouds. What about the complete opposite?"

"Might be adventure time," the fairy whispered to me.

I thought it might be in my better interest to know just what Santa was thinking.

"Ho, ho, you want to know?" Santa asked, hearing my thoughts.

"First, I will need to find the sleigh," he murmured.

He pulled a telephone from his deep pocket and punched numbers. He asked where the Santa sleigh was located. *Oh. Only half a world away!*

"Good," he said. You could be here in less than two minutes."

And it was! One minute, fifty-seven seconds! It was immediately hovering slightly below the trees and just above the water. Eight enormous reindeer and Santa's large sleigh practically filled all visible space!

"Come down here," Santa kindly called, waving his arm gently in our direction.

The sleigh descended slowly to be just low enough for me to step aboard and sit, once again, in Santa's enormous seat.

The fairy wanted to follow, and so she did. She said that an adventure sounded exactly like what she wanted on this particular day. She was ready for whatever was coming.

Santa somewhat loudly spoke to the Lead'Deer, "Adventure trip, maybe? You know, *just the opposite sort of thing*. What do you think?"

She slowly nodded, looked a little nervous, but led the sleigh forward. Silently and smoothly, we seemed to glide above the canal for a short distance to a small bridge. Gracefully, we curved upward and flew over tall trees to the river that runs alongside the canal.

The Delaware River, as it flows by us, is large, wide, and incredibly beautiful. We flew upstream staying about two feet above the rushing river when an opening appeared in the flow.

An opening? A hole in the river! Large, wide, and dark.

Bravely, the reindeer barrel-rolled and dove straight into the hole! We raced through the cool darkness to a large cavern. We could hear the river loudly rushing above.

I could feel my heart pounding. *But can you imagine? The Santa Claus sleigh with eight giant reindeer flying into a hole and under a river?* We sat onboard, holding our breath in the black void, as the sleigh sped forward. The tiny fairy lost a little of her sense of adventure and climbed into my shirt pocket for protection.

We continued to speed forward, then, suddenly, suddenly, *suddenly*, slowed and stopped! The deer slid sideways causing the sleigh to swing in a huge wide arc. The fairy and I held on tight as we bounced, scraped, and scratched to a final stop.

There was silence inside the huge, dark space, except for the distant roar of the river above.

I dared to open one eye. To my astonishment, the Santa sleigh lit up brightly! (The Santa Claus sleigh does these magical things. I have witnessed it before.) Our surroundings were revealed by the glowing sleigh.

Rocks, rocks, and more rocks. Shaped like storm clouds, they were hard, wet, and gray everywhere. *Rocks all around. Nothing but rocks.*

The deer looked nervously from left to right.

I called to Lead'Deer. She turned and admitted, "We don't know where we are. We haven't done this ever before. We can't see the stars above which usually guide us. We don't know where to turn."

"What a special, adventure place this is," I said, slightly frightened.

"We don't know where we are or where to go," the reindeer repeated helplessly.

We floated in the dark space, with the river above, the rocks below and all around, and the sleigh shining, halfway between the top and the bottom, halfway to the left, and halfway to the right and suspended in space but with no direction in the darkness.

Whoosh! Suddenly, bats flew at us from every direction. They flew into my head, bounced off my shoulders, and gripped tightly to the deer.

The bats were everywhere; a black cloud of them was surrounding us, blinding us. Chirping, chirping, and *chirping*.

The deer were scared and didn't know where to go or what to do.

The fairy emerged from the recesses of my pocket and positioned herself in front of my nose.

"I think I know the answer," she whispered.

The fairy flew forward. With a gentle touch, she guided the Lead'Deer straight ahead, then down onto the ground. The rest of the deer team followed. Happily, so did the sleigh and I.

"Which way is the air moving?" she asked.

The reindeer raised their noses, to sense, and pointed.

"We will walk into the breeze, however soft it might be," said the tiny heroine.

We slowly walked forward, bumping, pitching, and rocking.

After a not-so comfortable journey, we stepped suddenly into a wide meadow of tall grass, swaying in a warm breeze. We carefully moved toward the comforting rays of sunshine.

The bats disappeared.

We were completely surrounded and sheltered by the tall blades of grass. The sky above was delicate china blue. We continued forward, glad that this rather frightful adventure seemed to be over.

Or was it?

Suddenly, the ground dropped from beneath us. We fell, spiraling, through emptiness. The ground became sinking sand, falling quickly, rapidly. The reindeer fought to regain control, but the sleigh continued to dive. Sand poured around us and on us like a waterfall. We landed on a steep slope and found ourselves on the edge of a high cliff with a deep, deep valley below.

The sleigh took off from the cliff edge out into clear air and sunshine. A waterfall of sand spilled behind us into the deep valley.

Our reindeer slowed and paused in midair. Still covered with sand, they shook until not a grain was left on them. But the sleigh was still full, and its weight was dragging us downward.

In my life, I could not believe what I said next. I fear heights and have never been comfortable flying in Santa's open sleigh.

"Lead'Deer," I called, "could we, please, turn upside down to drain this sand out of the sleigh?"

She looked back at me, smiled, and nodded. She knew I really didn't want to flip over, but slowly, we did, and the sand poured out. The deer flew upside down and slowly forward. My head pointed toward the ground far below. I swallowed hard.

Suddenly…a mountain of ice appeared ahead. We drifted into and landed on it, upside down and floating!

It was very cold. The deer shivered hard. The fairy climbed back into my shirt pocket to find warmth.

Lead'Deer called to me, loudly, "At the North Pole, we stand on top of the ice. Now we are standing under it. Perhaps we might be at the South Pole."

"How can we be floating upside down on a huge slab of ice?" I asked.

"We have to find a warmer place," I added.

"A warmer place," Lead'Deer agreed to the direction.

The reindeer and sleigh took off with incredible speed, so fast that I could see history passing before us: Trojan horse, Boston tea party, landing on the Moon. I could see famous things happening before my eyes!

Suddenly…we found ourselves back where it all began, floating, upright, in midair, above the Delaware Canal. The evening was still warm.

I looked at my watch. *We landed an hour before we had taken off!*

"Adventure trips can have unexpected results," Lead'Deer said.

Santa Claus, however, was nowhere to be seen.

I stepped off the sleigh and walked to where my conversation started with the big man in the gray sweat suit.

There was no sign on the grass where he had been sitting.

I turned to look back at the wonderful golden reindeer and the magnificent sleigh hovering above the canal.

As I watched, the entire adventure transport became an array of colored floating snowflakes, which drifted slowly to the water and melted.

I was alone again, on the canal bank, with the smiling daffodils.

And so you see, my cousins, my dear Katie and Edward, there is much we could discuss about these happenings. I must tell you that I suspect the big fellow will show up again, but I have no idea when that may be.

I will certainly keep you informed.

My best,
Your cousin David